D1277941

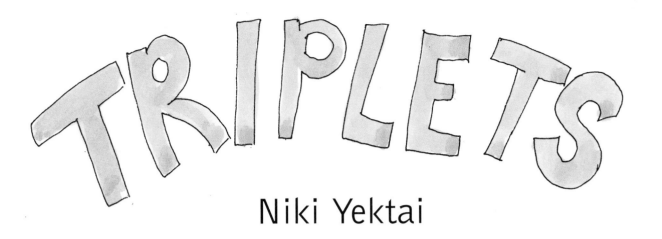

TRIPLETS

Niki Yektai

The Millbrook Press
Brookfield, Connecticut

For *my* twin, Maryellie K. Johnson

Yektai, Niki.
Triplets / Niki Yektai.
p.   cm.
Summary: Three boisterous sisters prove to be a handful for their
parents on a bus trip, at bathtime, and when they get frightened at
night.
ISBN 0-7613-0351-0 (lib. bdg.)   0-7613-0348-0 (pbk.)
[1. Triplets—Fiction. 2. Sisters—Fiction.] I. Title.
PZ7.Y376Tr 1998
[E]—dc21   97-23993   CIP   AC

Published by
The Millbrook Press
2 Old New Milford Road
Brookfield, CT 06804
5 4 3 2 1

Chapter One
BUS

Sophie, Aurelia, and Prue are on the bus with Mother.

"Are they triplets?" asks a lady.

"Yes," says Mother proudly.

"They are darling!"

"You deserve a medal, taking care of triplets!" exclaims a man.

"But they look <u>so</u> <u>good</u>!" everyone says.

"Thank you," says Mother.

The bus has stopped. When it starts again, Sophie, who is often the leader, says, "I wanna ring." She wants to press the tape that rings a bell and tells the bus driver to stop.

"Our stop isn't next," says Mother.

"I'm getting off," says a lady. "You can ring for me."

But now Aurelia wants to ring. "It's _my_ turn! Last time _you_ did it." She pushes Sophie off the seat and rings. "_Bing_!"

Sophie is crying.

"Now, Sophie, we're getting off soon," says Mother. "You'll ring then."

But Sophie punches Aurelia, and they start fighting on the floor.

People who have been saying how cute the triplets are have stopped saying it.

It's hard for Mother to separate Sophie and Aurelia, because Prue, the youngest triplet, is clinging to her. Prue is very clingy.

"We're almost at our stop," says Mother. "Someone must ring."

"My turn!" cries Prue. She elbows Mother and lunges for the bell. Too late. Sophie suddenly climbs on the seat and rings. "*Bing!*"

Now Prue's screaming. Still, she manages to kick Sophie, which starts Sophie screaming, too. Aurelia's having a tantrum on the floor. "WAAAAAAAAA!"

"Come on, girls!" says Mother. She gets off the bus with Prue upside down and red in the face.

Mother stands on the sidewalk.
A man hands her a screaming Aurelia.

Mother drops her on the sidewalk and goes back for Sophie, who is handed to her by a pretty girl.

Now that the triplets are off the bus, they lose their desire to ring. They stop bawling and walk home.

"I have never been so embarrassed in my life," says Mother.

At home she collapses in a chair.
Sophie has a bright idea. She whispers to her sisters.

"Sorry," they say to Mother.
They surround her and give her a
triplet kiss: Prue on top, Sophie on
the right, and Aurelia on the left.
SMACK! All at once.
"Oh," says Mother. "That's
three times nicer than a regular
kiss. My darling triplets."

Chapter Two
BATH

Aurelia is the naughty triplet. She's a difficult eater, too. She sits at the table and stores her meat in her cheek. She won't swallow it.

"You look like a chipmunk," says Father. "Kindly swallow. The steak is delicious."

When father isn't looking she transfers the meat to her pocket and later, the toilet.

At bath time it's Aurelia's idea to play cooking in the tub. "Let's cook something <u>good</u> for a change," she says.

She runs to get the pots.

"We're playing restaurant," she tells Mother.

"Oh, all right," says Mother.

Aurelia cooks chicken soup, using soap.
"Have some soup," she says.
"Yummy," says Prue.

Aurelia pretends to eat it.

"Yuk!" she says. "Too much chicken!"

She throws the whole potful onto the bathroom floor.

Then Sophie cooks a stew.
"Yuk! Too much smelly shrimp! Throw it away!" cries Aurelia.
Sophie dumps it out.

"Want some ice cream with hot fudge sauce?" asks Prue.
"Yuk! Too lumpy. Throw it out!" says Aurelia.
"Wheeeeeeeeee!" cries Prue.

WEEEEEE !

"Here's some spinach," says Aurelia.

"YUK!" say Prue and Sophie. Over it goes.

"—some cabbage!"

"YUK!"

"—some fish!"

"Get rid of it!"

The doorbell rings. It's Mrs. Oppenheimer who lives in the apartment below.
"It is raining in my living room," she says.
"What could you possibly mean by that?" asks Father. "It can't rain inside."
"Humph!" says Mrs. Oppenheimer. "Are the triplets having a bath?"
She marches to the bathroom.

When she opens the door, water pours out.

Mother and Father mop, and the triplets help, too.

"The restaurant had bad food," explains Aurelia.

Even if Aurelia had a good excuse, Mother and Father are too angry to listen.

They go downstairs
with Mrs. Oppenheimer.
For a few minutes
longer there is a light
drizzle in her living room.
But Sophie, Aurelia,
and Prue are not allowed
to see.

Chapter Three
BED

Prue can't sleep. She makes the mistake of looking under her bed and sees something in the shadows, which is a wet towel and some socks.

"A monster's under the bed!" she cries.

"Monsters aren't real," says Sophie.

"Go to sleep and be quiet," says Aurelia.

But Aurelia's foot touches Sophie's furry slipper, which has been left on her bed. Aurelia kicks it.

"Prue! I <u>felt</u> it! A furry monster!" cries Aurelia. "I kicked it off the bed. Didn't you hear it land?"

"Y–y–y–yes," stammers Prue.

"Monsters aren't real," says Sophie. "Be quiet!"

A little later Sophie dreams about a furry monster prowling throughout the house. She sits up. "Maybe there <u>is</u> a monster in the room!" she cries.

"Aurelia...?"
No answer.
"Prue...?"
No answer.
They are not in their beds.
Sophie runs down the hall to
Mother and Father's room.

After awhile Father says, "Move over," to Mother.

"I'm not touching you," says Mother.

"Oh, it's one of the triplets," says Father, peering at Aurelia between them.

He stretches out.

"Owwww!" cries Sophie, who has been kicked in the head.

"There are a lot of people in this bed," says Father.

Mother turns over.

Thump!

"Is that you, Prue, on the floor? Are you all right?" asks Mother.

"You must all go back to your own beds," says Father.
"There's a monster in our room," say the triplets.
"WAAAAAAA!"
"Now don't be silly," says Mother, yawning. "You're just scaring each other. Monsters aren't real."

"We're very tired," says Father. "Go back to bed.
You'll be fine. Go to sleep, sweeties. Go on!"

Since the triplets don't move, he repeats, "Go on.
Go back to bed. Go to sleep. Go on!"

The triplets stop at the door.

"Go on. Go back to sleep."

"I know what to do," whispers Sophie.

Later Father gets up to go to the bathroom. He stumbles on something and flies across the hall.

"Why, it's the triplets," he mumbles on his hands and knees. "Looks like they've moved half their bedroom out here. Sophie—Aurelia—Prue—Hello— Do you mind leaving a passage to the door?"

No one answers.

When Father returns from the bathroom, he places his feet very carefully here and there on the girls' quilts. Still, Sophie kicks him.

Then she mumbles in her sleep, "Go back to bed. Go to sleep. Go on!"

"Thank you, I'll try," says Father.